A HUNGER FOR THE FLYING

EXPLORATIONS OF AN ORDINARY SOUL

Poetry from the
Second Half of a Life

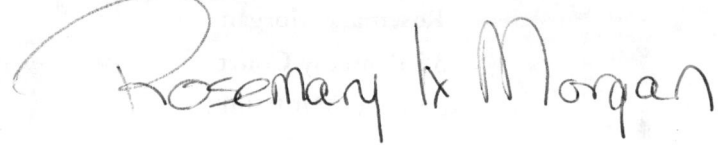

BY

ROSEMARY IX MORGAN

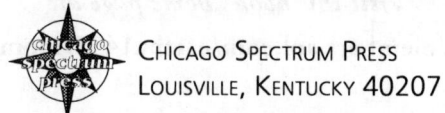

CHICAGO SPECTRUM PRESS
LOUISVILLE, KENTUCKY 40207

©1998 by Rosemary Ix Morgan

 CHICAGO SPECTRUM PRESS
4848 BROWNSBORO CENTER
LOUISVILLE, KENTUCKY 40207

Additional copies may be purchased by sending $14.95 plus $4 shipping and handling (check or money order) to:
Rosemary Morgan
35 Pomeroy Court
Amherst, MA 01002

Printed in the U.S.A.

10 9 8 7 6 5 4 3 2 1

ISBN: 1-886094-89-6

Visit this book's home page at:
http://members.aol.com/eartha1435/mom.htm

This book is dedicated to all those
who seek to live from the heart

GRAY

*

Every mother's child is born hungry   lusting for life
for milk of gentleness   for touching
for laughter and for holding hands
we come in trailing joy like the tail on a kite
but they have scissors here on earth   sharp things
branches   and a very crafty breeze
we are impaled and torn

How did we earn the coming to this planet?
the pain   I can't believe it all just started here
what went before?
we have been sentenced   we turn gray with pain
Earth is where the gray ones must decide
to open up and learn   or die

This planet is about distinctions
how could we know the meaning of together
who never walked alone   and yet
it's not about black and white   it's about seeing gray
and knowing that underneath the gray in anyone
there lies a heart which dreams of rainbows
and a hunger for the flying

CONTENTS

❧

🌹 RAINBOWS

❦

THE HUNGER

INTRODUCTION

I am willing when we meet
to see who you are
now

And I don't need a pedigree
or references
they might hide the you I want to know

I won't rely on outward signs
of what you are
you're surely more or less
than these will show

I will not ask
what you possess
but wonder what the having means to you

I'll not ask accomplishments
or failures
they might tempt me backward
into judgment

I'll try to shed pretense for you
and show you what I care about today
what I want to care about
is you

But I am still unlearning things
and slip sometimes
I hope that you will want to understand

So show me who you really are
as best you can
I'm hoping for a friend to share the road

THE SILVER SPOON

Black Starr and Gorham   Fifth Avenue   1956
pre-nuptial dream comes true
my mother looks important   always does

Deep rugs   expensive quiet   burnished cases
filled with treasure   eager hands presenting
opulence in tableware   etched
hammered   molded
sharp-edged utensils fit to tell the world
from whence I came and who I soon would be

Amazing how that dream-filled eye slid by
the intricacy and made for dollar show
to rest upon a spoon   the pattern *Frontier Plain*
high polished gentle curve   the absence of pretense
the shape is the design   I choose congruity
despite exasperated whispers
"It's not important enough!"

Oh Mom   it's not important now
that we chose different ways   the spoon

did show the scratches just the way you said it would
    but sitting here   I'm glad I held my ground
back then   I couldn't know that I'd be melted down
        to simple lines myself

       Your burning came from radiation
  two years told the tale   before the end
    I saw the splendid silver core of you
  and read forgiveness in your blue gray eyes
today   the spoon reminds me of the journey
    out of pretense   into simple loving

SIBLINGS

Can a fish befriend a fox
or bird
we were that different
alien one to another
held together by genetics
held apart by jealousy and competition
held together by advantages
held by   tantalized by
that seldom visitor
the possibility of love

SHORT REPRIEVE

A Memory

Safe and lost in a grove of pine
the awkward child forgets herself   sits down
half-smile plays on parted lips
she is a mermaid near the bottom of the sea
floating lazily in the emerald air
a fairy safe in stalks of giant meadow grass
a giant fe-fi-fumming over mountains made of moss

She breathes out pain
breathes in pure pine faintly astringent
sees a squirrel hesitate then move
the whole black world in one curved eye
hears a furtive car whisper ineffective epithets
at the edge of the glen
then peace comes down again like winter snow

Her fingers find the tiny clubs of moss
small barriers to the scurrying spider
moving through the forest inch by inch

Her cheek finds softness in the moss
her eye rises up to a star-shaped piece of sky
and somewhere near a small bird sings

SUPERMARKET STUPEFACTION

❧

For Grace

Imitation margarine!
they needed to achieve it?
now just show me anything
and maybe I'll believe it

Today it's imitation this
and imitation that
they've got an imitation
for imitation fat

Well!   imitation margarine
is bastardized butter
and I told the dairy manager
I'd rather have the *udder!*

FOG

Do you suppose
when minds whir too fast
with undone plans
oughts and ifs
and hurryings to nothing
fog comes?

Giant comforter
to mute the clacking brain
and whisper to the sated senses
easy now   and   gently dear

When eyes are dimmed
see with the heart
the wisdom of a quiet time
to pause and sense direction

THAW

If my love
like the sun
could melt the snow
imprisoning a barren heart
just perhaps
that mud warm earth
might blossom

ODD TREE ME

Odd tree me   —   to beg for pruning!
I do not lust for knife edge
or glory in pain
but celebrating life
I long to use my strength
for budding

SAND PIT MEDITATION

I am the hillside
ravaged by the 'dozer of rigidity
gullied by the rain of tears
waiting now for seeds within
to cover me in blossoms

INVISIBLE SEED

I was hidden on the earth
stay dry
stay cold
stay safe

I felt the sun and rain
and dared to swell for sprouting
only to catch the eye
of a hungry bird

DEPRESSION

✿

Yesterday   forever ago
the world shone with beauty
was it real?
all drenched in stained-glass glow
have I smashed that window
with thoughts I dared to think?

I walk a wasteland   forced on
by the anguish of the present
eyes downward   on mud
made of tears and the dust of old dreams
longing for order and peace within
so hungry for beauty that
I grab shards out of the mud
ignoring how I bleed

ICE STORM MEDITATION

We are boughs of winter tree
bound in ice of daily oughts
brought low to earth by fearsome weight
begging only not to break

and yet   without the ice
who could guess the glory
after sunrise in the forest

I AM

I draw apart
to silence
and wonder who
I am

I travel
out of history
in now
I am

Beyond my name
and naked
of activity
I am

Receiving life
and sensing
possibility
I am

TIME PUSHES ME ON

Time pushes me on
into the spiral of tomorrow
my body
weighted with the sense of now
is not reluctant
but lingers
pleased to be alive
content to savor dreams
which will become
the yet unknown
reality

LEHRKIND MANSION

Still stiff-spined
with sagging jowls
she sat receiving callers
and reigning vague-eyed over nothing
a senile   soup-stained   semi-invalid with
audible gastric distress
a remnant of her small town aristocracy

But then I saw the laugh lines
webbed about her watering eyes
and old tree hands   once useful

And gently
not to pain her
I began to comb the tangles
from her hair

I BATHED IN MOONLIGHT

The rusted metal shower is all that's left
other fixtures   curtains   and the moldings
from those long windows are gone

Still at night I come   undress by dim reflected light
get plaster dust between my toes   shiver nipples tight
and enter at a touch through those complaining doors

Heat   sharp and total on my back and dinning on the tin
expel the tension of another day and clean away
mistakes and dirt

Last night again   the ritual   but very late
and strange   that only slowly I perceived
the moonlight and the moon full bright
within the naked window frame

I opened up the groaning doors
and puddling the ancient floor
I became young   and Greek   and watched
the diamonds dripping on the softness of my breast

THIS LOAF

I am grateful for this loaf of bread
all brown and warm simplicity
not gourmet fare   but nourishing
hand made to no one's recipe
I eat it now with quiet thanks
for I have lived on less

HANGERS

I suspect
that I'm correct
that in the closet
I deposit
twisted wires
with desires

Day or night
in absence of light
they cannot wait
to copulate
so hanging loose
they reproduce

I open the door
and always find more
in bunches and tangles
are more fertile angles

I wish I could catch 'em
before they could hatch 'em

AUTUMN PRAYER

Let me
like a leaf
live my life
anonymously
productive for my tree

and then exhaust myself
with splendid color

LAUNDRY

Living life
is rather like
doing wash
— it's always there

Tangled impressions I need to sort
new ideas to test for shrinking
worn ideas   like tired socks
for me to set aside
resolves   I starch like shirts
(lest I appear limp before the world)
moods to deal with   non-colorfast
odd colors changing all the wash against my will

Heaven'll be   no laundry for me
but the end of the chore
when it's all in the drawer

COME OUT COME OUT
WHEREVER YOU ARE

Busy-ness bolsters the roles I play
accomplish so all may see
busy-ness fills up an empty day
and hides me quite well from me

Courage is needed to say to myself
it's quiet now you can come out
but it's good and we talk and conjecture
on just what life's all about

And I see in myself how I need to grow
it's surprising that I'm so small
if I hadn't put busy-ness by for a bit
I might never have seen it at all

GLUTTONY

I think
even old ladies at tea parties
really care
who gets the chocolate one

OBSERVATION

I'm sick unto death of trying to be
what somebody else wants to see
living with judgment is not to be free
to hell with the judge at least I like me

SNOWSHINE

Astringent air and
gentle darkness
of this winter night
draw me
from the children's chatter
supper smells and warmth
to silence

Snow crystals glitter
capturing the street lamp shine
glorious in a fraction of time
and then are dark again
and glitter lies elsewhere
in the snow

And I see people
living   for an instant
reflecting God
in time

SPECULATION

What if
stars are cells
floating in the serum space
of some gigantic knowing one

And I
a virus on this planet earth
unaware
that I effect cosmos
so small that I cannot conceive
the titan of existence

MACROSCOPIC CYTOLOGY

More often than I care to say
I move amoeba-like
sensing warmth   or needs
til now unrecognized
a part of me leaps out to meet
existence specks   realities
as they float by
and I absorb them hungrily
ignoring how I shape
the me I will become

JOURNEY OUT OF ORTHODOXY

Or is Becoming Really the Point?

Once I was Pinnochio
moved by my Gipetto God
and all was well until
a cricket told me God was more
and so was I

And I set out with him
to find a God who was enough
and ways to make me real

And we search everywhere
and stop to eat
freedom for breakfast
and fear for dinner nightly

I see the cricket growing
but   am I

or

in the end will I be
some

strange

        mutant

      ridin

   giant

cricket

  zig

      zag

to a walled estate
with giant gate
marked
PUPPETS

ROOTS

I hear the roots of me
tangled fibers of an unseen multitude
reaching back in time through ages of soil
hidden   black   cool
all the way to the rock of nothingness
which once was
and I hear
you now!
in the sun!
flower
for us!
and I
sing yes!
and
feel
buds
c
o
m
i
n
g
!

SCISSORS AND SHARP THINGS

ON APPROACHING CRISIS

Let me take the sand of nows
and wash it carefully in my mind
discarding imperfection

Let me polish stones of tiny joys
and scrub the ordinary clean
to gleam from each direction

Let me greet the coming fire
bravely   knowing I await
crystal resurrection

RAGE COME AND GONE

Anger's scorching footprints pound
across my mind
branding the tranquility as false
the thunder stomping in my ears recedes
acrid stench of failure all around and
I am left with tears to quench fires

DROUGHT

Hot breezes torture meadow grass
the sole reply is desolation's rustle
leaf curls in upon itself
fading green and crumbling at a touch
earth splits wide   a female
begging for the moist relief of love

OPTIMISM

I will move
without luxuriously certainty
some may say
I move with doubts   and foolishly

I would say
I move in faith   and willingly
to reach a goal
I dare leave undefined

A SMALL PIECE OF THE PUZZLE

Everything is paradox
nothing is what it seems
indeed rare flowers rise from dung

LIKE DYING

Birds fly low and fast
leaves are wind-herded
to a resting spot
low clouds move east
in silence
sun fingers heading west
stroke the fallow field
and disappear

I ONLY SEE WHAT I SEE

Fire tongues naked
on the gentle winds of autumn
shimmer
gold and scarlet

Afterbirth
of rigid waxen stem
pushed out   milimeter by milemeter
in slow motion
by promises of
tomorrows multiplying
silently

There is nothing fragile or
tender in this dying season
only stubborness bruised
endurance flaunting itself
against murderous odds

By night by day
the very earth itself
shudders
with the effort to live

ON GRIEF

This first day is
a spider web
laid against the wound
by a wise old
Indian woman

She says nothing
and I see in her dark eyes
tomorrow and tomorrow
more webs

until one day
like a dry leaf
the scab will fall away

RAY'S PIECRUST

I had a neighbor once named Ray
retired teacher labeled gay by those most certain
of their own orientation

He was a little odd   dyed his hair auburn
sometimes gave himself a perm and
hoed his garden while he wore pink plastic curlers

I was finishing a marriage at the time
and raising little kids   ex-debutante
planted in Montana with survival skills to learn

I put in beans and spinach and potatoes
(forever ending my concern about dying of starvation
after nuclear attack in a Long Island potato field)

Our gardens were close by   though
mine would have fit in the pocket of his
we'd nod across the dusty alley   then we'd wave

While I corralled the trikes one day we spoke
he liked the kids and cooking and gardening
was rather like a maiden aunt   long past sixty

He had pasty English skin   sad brown eyes
    was pigeon-breasted   paunchy   lonely
and I was performing life-saving surgery   on myself

We graduated to coffee in the kitchen   he shared a recipe
for piecrust   with egg   and vinegar   and it froze well
    I never said I wanted it for quiche

Shortly after I was free he knocked at my back door
   with a bunch of beets   and not five minutes in
    he grabbed my waist and kissed me

Weirder than a duck singing Verdi   worse yet all I could say
    with school marm's finger wagging was
  that   *is a no-no!*   (so much for survival skills)

I've made a lot of pies since then   and think of him
and lessons learned   like   things aren't what they seem
    and don't believe the neighbor's gossip

RESOLUTION

I will not be again
aggressor
taking joy in power struggle
aiming blows and causing pain
savoring the victory to come

It came
and turned to gall
and I am left
relieved to find
I bruise vicariously

WOMAN ALONE

I walk a windswept way
cross barren land
and search at scudding clouds
to sense direction
choosing at the forks   because
the children walk behind

We go slowly now
against a piercing wind
and stop at night
by firelight
to eat   and dream
of home

THE VOICE

I barely hear the quiet voice
which says
be still

a third eye blinks
clear focused
sees

Consider everything   nothing
is irrelevant
still motion is the way

IT'S ALL IN THE MIND

the earth's
an aging whore
painted garrishly with autumn

no
don't say that
say

she is the only
reliable truth
right beneath my feet

SOUL PULSES FITFULLY WITHIN

Soul pulses fitfully within
trapped by flesh
folded   pressed down
weighted by everything worldly
the noise   and curiosity
constant distraction   even then
this core can swell
and come alive to rarity
beyond control of will
and to no clock it moves
and I am part of universe
vessel of the timeless
knowing and being
one

I HAVE STOOD FOR EONS

I have stood
for eons on the ocean brink
magma ejected from hell
startled by sunlight and
frozen thus
jagged
exposed

Capricious God
is playing statue games with me
while ages and the sea
work changes on my face
with rise and fall and rise

Come dancing restless womb
to welcome me again
and draw me
into deep green silence
me
smooth as pearl
someday before eternity

BROKEN DAY

Dawn   and sunshine pouring down my hill
puddling the garden   I sip coffee
watching peace

I hear chicadee distress
and mocking crow's call   where?
there   a dog fight in my sky

they buzz the black marauder recklessly
he   clumsy   weights a dew wet branch
and lumbers into hiding in that emerald world

nervous wings are useless in a tree
and screeching rage
is just futility
crow laughs   and hops a time or two
then nightmare slow he rises with
a hatchling in his beak
their bravery is not enough
they dive and swoop in spirals
across the meadow into day

do birds mourn?   I want to know
can air wars be erased
with another bug for breakfast?

perhaps they know Zen
and live only moment to moment to moment
dear God   let it be so

I STAND HIP DEEP AND WONDER

Am I a creature of the land or sea?
I stand hip deep and wonder
trusting earth and stones
those solid orienting things
beneath my feet
that speak in silence
of up and down and
the way from here to there
and certainty

I wish to be a keen-eyed runner
covering vast distances   straight-lined
and faster than the wind
so they would say   "How could she have?"
or else   "I never would have guessed she could!"
And I would be
the only one to trust with vital secrets
needed in Rome by morning
pumping through the night   merciless
I know my strength
deaf to muscle screamings   I arrive
and they are saved by my unfailing will

REDEMPTION

Can someone
tell me please
what's real

The books of wisdom say
seek God   the real is unreal
less is more

I wriggle mole blind
search out tubers
claw toward pearly grub

surface dawn and dusk
near sightless
in the half-light times

to savor
where I do not quite belong
and can never stay

What is
redemption
to a mole?

And if I am a mole
why do I dream
of burial

on a platform
bright with feathers
in a tree?

MID-DAY   LOW TIDE

My body   made of wax   is softening
    mouth opens   wanting to pant
        nerves pull eyelids to slits
        to check a jaundiced sky

Gray satin   rhythmed   and comforting
    moves indifferently against the shore
        a shrugging shoulder or
    the breath of an old woman sleeping

ON HOPING TO FALL
IN LOVE AGAIN

She said what I would like the very best
before I die
is a bluebird of my very own to love

If I can find a bluebird
that will make my life worthwhile
because   I had a robin once and for a while
that was very nice
but a bluebird would be better

And so she lived
looking out the window   watching and
every now and then she'd go running after one
without success   but being a determined soul
she switched to going daily over fields
and through the pines   looking
harder   faster   further

But she never saw
the moss she crushed beneath her feet
or smelled the pines
or felt the sun because after all

she was looking for a bluebird of her very own
to make her life worthwhile

Nor welcomed rain after dusty days
nor caught a snowflake on her tongue
nor felt the peace of rocking by the fire
nor scratched the dog
whose satin eyes were filled with her

All because she spent it
looking for a bird that never came

POPPY

Sea-green hairy
ovoid splits
disclosing scarlet woman

Tight-fisted from restraint
she bursts
wrinkled into day

Relaxes from the effort of
a birth gone well
beneath an unrelenting sun

Smooths out her up-turned petticoats
nods barely
to the sniggered whisper of a breeze

And smiles
exposing at her center
the joy of black

With every touch
even of the

wind

She bruises
fades to tan
torn tissue

Leaving behind
only the memory of
sensuality

SEPTEMBER PRAYER

Here and now is Genesis
creation time
a new year   clean books
sharp pencils   high hopes

Creator be with me
as I make my life
in this new place   and choose
a hundred times a day

Be here as I struggle
and try to grow
help me to learn from my mistakes
let me never build my success
upon another's pain
remind me of the special gifts
you've given me to share

Help me to believe in you
and in me
and to remember that
now I am creating
myself and my future

SUGAR TIME

Tree stands pierced
and oozing spring
so life-filled
and bursting
that any cut at all
will tell the tale
right on the street
in public

SUNDAY ON THE PORCH

A rippling wind fragments the farmer's voice
from field where May-time haying has begun

Again this year the crow is on attack
he fancies fledglings for a noontime meal

The air slides past this shaded space to spin
suspended coleus flagrant in its pot

The purple finch up-ends itself to drink
then mounts an unseen stairway to the tree

A sensate cat parades the living lawn
her footprints made in single file

I take it all in   as
cell by cell the hay begins to rise

MILK OF GENTLENESS

FORTY PLUS

A log being consumed
shoots spark surprises
and hisses secret messages

It lies heat-gouged into almost rectangles
half gone   shimmering   fracturing in slow motion
into weightless lumps   gray as old snow

Such a tiny piece of time in which to glow

Fire tender prods it near another
it will not flame alone
fire lives in the narrow space between

Before I am cold and scattered by the wind
let God's hands be warm   and light dance
in those all-seeing eyes

NIGHTMARE

The fear is
I'll frighten you
the way you frighten me
because   I've left my reason far behind
like yesterday's shirt upon the floor
while I run naked down the street
after you

I've kept a citadel for years
built of   oh wells   and   I cans
a bulwark with flower boxes
and crisp curtains at the windows
and I forgot the pain
and then through leaded glass I saw you pass
and throwing wide the door
I ran to catch you round the bend

Because if I saw right   I think
that I'd be safe with you
and you would be the first   maybe ever
to love me as I really am

and dry my tears   and calm my fears
    and hold me all night long

But will I frighten you away?   and
    having come this far
do I remember where I used to live?

WE

We have begun
a gentle time
of little things
shared

your eyes
your touch explain
I do not need to be
afraid

I wear peace
like a shawl
because
you came

FINDERS KEEPERS

A Poem to His Old Girlfriend

She roamed thin coated   bone cold
against a nasty wind
looking amid the chaos
for something
anything of value

Yesterday
she found a pretty piece
perhaps   she thought
and carried it a while
but saying no she set it down
and went her way
the emptiness a greater pain

I sat at fireside   safe warmed
carefully writing inquiries
for something that would be
appropriate   when looking up
I spied what she had left
and fetched it to my mantlepiece
where it shines uncommonly

Odd   and unfair

that she who casts herself
upon the world wholeheartedly
has nothing now
and I   cautious
and rather small of spirit
possess the prize

I do intend to guard it with my life
even against her   and yet
I want to call her sister saying
rest a bit with me   have tea
be warm

but ungenerously I would have to say
please
sit with your back to the mantle

TOUCH

Before hearing   or sight   the avenue to understanding
was touch
to test the boundaries of the womb

Now mid-life   once more understanding nothing
we touch wordless   to tell what can't be said
(the thought has not been made)

We are twins
half-formed
exploring in love

I have not yet a sense that these waters
lap at any walls at all
and the message skin to skin   is peace

THE DOUBLE BED

Each night
I find the gift
I thought I'd lost
at birth

A primal safety
warmth
with two hearts beating
to lead me into dreaming

Without effort
I am nourished while I sleep
and born again each morning
at a touch

COFFEE HOUSE JAZZ

❧

Sound drowned   I found me
alone walled in by rhythmed noise
Where is Ommmmm-soft silence   peace?
cacophony surrounds abounds around
that quiet piece of me that wants
to go home Ommmmm or
talk with you outside the rhythm
random raunch that teases wheezes sucks
seduces you while I smile
mother patient
waiting
inundated by undulating sound

HIS LIPS

Sometimes   this old man's mouth takes on an innocence
as if he'd never tasted nicotine or gin
as if the jungle in his head had somehow become
an ordered English garden where everything belonged
and nothing was extra

This proud man who would not stoop to please
this cautious habitual man   prone to regularities
whose mind wrestles dragons while his mouth speaks
the thoughts of other men   necessities and courtesies
and then is still   comes into momentary balance
like a child on a slender wall

Then his lips are perfect as a child's
who's never lied   they seem as scrubbed as a Dutch stoop
they are exquisitely sensual   free of sexuality
the line curves softly as an ear listening
curves perfectly   like the breast of a mocking bird
curves not full like a spinnaker in the wind
but gently   as the line of a hull flowing aft from the bow

He seems suddenly ready to make pure music
on a flute   or newly shriven   fit to pray
I fill myself with secret slippings of my eyes
to him and off again and back
until these lines are etched in me forever

STEPPENCAT

You know how   when you try to turn
an automatic car in too small a space
and the front wheels screech at you?
he purrs like that   only little

You know how when you're fishing
and your mind is absolutely elsewhere
and you get a sudden strike?   Well
he has fish hooks in the pockets of his feet

I remember when I was nine and running
I knew   if I ran just a little faster
I would fly   I tried   but didn't
he loves his body that way   and still tries

When I wear my fuzzy bathrobe and am still
he comes nibbling and kneading
home to mamma
exploring for a teat

He searches kitchen cabinets
or any womb dark cavity
with darting eyes
the way I search for God

ADVICE TO A FRIEND AT WORK

Life is risky
love is riskier
it means becoming vulnerable
and maybe getting hurt
going for the brass ring
fully aware that you may fall off the carousel and
bleed a lot and limp a bit and end up with a scar
or
get the brass ring

But friend be warned
if you risk not very much
not very much
is just what you'll probably get

OLD DOG'S NEW TRICKS

Her step is tentative upon the earth
long ago she could have been taken by an eagle

could have been clawed and bloodied
for another's sustenance

or frozen in a winter storm except we have the habit of
protecting her who once protected us

how did exuberance dwindle to seldom thumpings of a tail
and exactly when did silence wall her off

her eyes are clouded with perplexity   we are
sometimes strangers   eagle   wolf   a startling enemy

we walk too fast about the house
on an erratic course which baffles her

too inept course corrections
yield chaos underfoot

and when we let her in
she pees out her relief

forgets her shame and scratches
to get out again

even air has turned on her
become unwelcome guest to fluid in her lungs

she cannot quite recall
the feeling of a friendly hand

it's getting so she expects
only trouble and

she's dying of surprises

DISTINCTIONS

FULL MOON

Thirteen times a year
the waxing moon sends secret messages
small body hairs become antennae
transmitting rebellion

my molecules reverse themselves in orbit
speed up   slow down   who knows?

lunar energy jiggles chromosomes
gravitational aberrations short circuit memory
the skin wears thin   is flailed away
by idle comments masquerading as indictment

solid places fracture
feet grow eyes and still they try
to plant themselves in nothingness
in the spaces between the words

the liquid mind becomes gelatinous
crystallizes half-formed jumbled thoughts
into grandiose ice sculpture
fit only for a poem

HER NAME WAS JEANNIE

Only one generation before my own   in Vermont
a girl in love became pregnant
her father gave the baby away to be adopted
and had the doctor tie his daughter's tubes

Later the couple married but were childless
searched and found their daughter
thirteen years later   after she had been abused
they tried to help but could not change what had been done

But when this mother could   she made a loving bed
by the fire in the basement of her home for her niece
who was in love with a young man   and gave the two of
them
a gentler start to loving

And the niece told me how her aunt and uncle
sought each other always   with eyes   with hands
in crowds and all alone   because
what else did they have?

But when her aunt was taken by cancer
her uncle took another wife in three months' time

LAYOFFS

There is a hatchet in the hen house
frantic know-nothings smell the danger
when a chicken is beheaded
even the cows give sour milk

HOLDING HANDS

After we have been stiff-necked
hands are the go-between
they finger air with subtlety
to find each other as we walk
we each pretend the little touch means nothing
but the smallest finger link means
there's hope

And on an ordinary day my hand
finds and fits into his own
surely   the way a captain
brings a ship to port   or
with gratitude   the way a weary bird
settles on the nest

COMFORT

❧

I

In the time of need its absence was brailled
without comprehension   (the starving primitive
cannot conceive New Zealand apples in spring)
dreams at best a milky gruel
survives on God knows what
grows thin-boned and used to hunger
determined when the babies come
to give what never was received

II

How could I paint what I never saw?
abstractly with the colors of my intent
with blotches of mistaken graspings
spills of excess   whorls of wonder

I know now I never was an expert in this art
I stand before my mural holding out a little frame
between its vastness and my eye searching
for smaller spaces pleasingly designed

TODAY'S ANSWERS

Do I love you?
Am I loved?
What is love anyway?

Love doesn't limit
love turns us loose

Love comes in pieces
like tinker toys
or an erector set

We build toward one another
and over time
the pieces span the distance

From me to you
a splendid bridge
with lights

THE THREE OF THEM

They walk all over him
with arrogance   deliberately
nonchalantly   at a whim
they stake their claim
demand   expect   wheedle   cry
every waking moment

With only rare exasperation
he tends
their bodies' needs   their hearts' desire
his hand would never raise against them
who offer love to him creatively
in the language of his heart

He loves them perfectly   accepts
their claws and midnight shrieks
cleans up the stains
and Hoovers up the endless cat hair
as any gentle father would
he says they are my children

RESPONSIBILITY

It's Sunday Evening   peaceful
barely raining
I see the neighbor's little ones squatting
under a rainbow umbrella
sheltering month old bunnies in a cage
contemplating their responsibility

I contemplate my cats   and last month's
fetal rabbit on my doorstep
hating violence   loving tulips
I am perplexed
about my own responsibility

CHINESE CALLIGRAPHY

Tell me brush strokes deftly made
of the world behind the careful hand
which flicked you into being
what thought does absent spirit send to me?

does passion speak here?
no   gladness   something optimistic
a woman on a road somewhere
glad to be going   not knowing where

Jaunty stepper whistles at the moon
makes a breeze in miniature
lost in ink black air
the curves of her salute the night
the band around her breast contains a pride
born of persistence   constant yes
to possibility

Her arms encircle everything
excepting nothing   not trial
nor sorrow   regret nor failure   everything
is what it is   everything falls of itself

like grain into a basket   so the latest gift
(the moonlight glinting in a puddle) falls
beside an ancient ache
and these hull-less gifts become as equals
cancelling the basket to a weightless burden

MIDDLE AGE

I was born adult   and worrying
and grew in wisdom and aridity
until surprised
I feel a raindrop quicken me

Soul stirs
to rhythm borning on my graying head
ordered firmament softens to ooze
roots suck

I swell
and for my golden birthday
give myself
a childhood

COMING INTO BALANCE

They never taught in school
the other sense which grows mid-life

to heal a left brained weariness
an ear-shaped fungus sending root threads deep

I weaken from its feeding imperceptibly
and I will die but need not have it otherwise

for that new sense gives ample sustenance of peace
delight in mud   the breeze   crow's call
a black November branch
slimming into lace too fragile for a queen

I hear and see the pasture and the sky
and gazing into that need nothing more

THAT I SHOULD BE PRIVY TO KNOW!

Written in response to a telecast of Nature
seen on Thanksgiving evening, 1986

Once in every year   after rain
floods the river meandering through
the Pantanal in southwestern Brazil
an undistinguished apple snail rises by night
from the bottom muck

It surfaces   floating on the current
until it can adhere with its foot
to a suitable stalk rising from the flood
then climbs to a specific height which
it perceives to be safe above the water

Protected only by the humid air of night
it spreads itself wide in ultimate vulnerability
and opens a place in its liverish self
to exude a slippery matrix which
runs a channel across flesh to twig

At a slugly pace   a single white egg
emerges on the slimy track

is shifted by dint of sensate undulating flesh
at last it clings to the twig
held by slime   thickening to glue

Again   a multitude of times   an egg
slips along in good snail time
to bend itself efficiently into a hexagon which hugs
its sibling neighbors

On the twig by moonfall
the white cluster is oblong
complete and drying
deaf to minor plop of weary snail
rejoining water

In air by day the nest hardens
to off-white insignificance
life stirs   pulses   swims   brews
in its own juices

In time   walls within the nest wither
from the friction of activity
weight of growth measured in microns
snailets move together in a common pool
at the base of the weakening nest

From which one drop gathers
oozes free   and another until
pearled in amniotic fluid

a speck of transparent glistening life
clad in helicidaen perfection waits

Falls at last to another water
where pure alchemy
turns the shell instantly solid   safe
and then it slowly sinks in muck

THE VERY CRAFTY BREEZE

FOR AIDES

❧

To the residents of a nursing home, aides are the most important people.
Where I used to work, most of the nurses referred to the aides as "kids"

Draw the line
against those who say
you are expendable
replaceable
dime a dozen kids
who gain experience
and then go on

You are women
all ages and stages
living out the lives you have
as best you can

Stand upon your worth
because you give
what others can't or won't

You look deeply into sorrow
and smile and touch
and daily cup your hands

106

to blow upon the sparks of lives
delivered here like ashes in a sack

You are
life-givers in a dying house
don't let them call you
kids

WOMAN OF MEANS

Wide-eyed   subtly apprehensive
when she came she made it plain
she was used to the best
which we just happen to offer
and which   in this case
or any other really
isn't good enough

She took the tour
in a wheel chair
and given available alternatives
decided we would do

DOE

She lived alone   a past unknown to me   except
she worked and put her aunt here years ago
and with her sister visited and cared for her until
Doe herself lost her job   her mind unraveled
with increasing speed   she couldn't cook
and the restaurant closed   so Doe went begging
to the neighbors for some food
they called the sister who evolved the plan

They came to visit Auntie   Doe was made to stay
what can be said when the memory of the moment past is
gone?
enraged thoughts flew too fast to catch in words
and she could not defend herself from starched efficiency
which patronized and tied her down and fed her pills
until she wet herself and walked like a drunk
and the agitation was somewhat controlled

A reasonable request   incontinent and barely walks
that's such a change   could we suggest
the doctor lower meds and work to get her up again

She sits hands tensed around a small table top
which ties her to the chair
leaning sideways head cocked as if to catch
a phantom conversation or a waiter's eye
except her eyes are closed deliberately and
the only waiters here are waiting for something else

I sit and talk to her and take her hand   throat sounds
say yes and no   two octaves low
she does not move at all
her legs are rag doll limp   her torso stiff
I talk some more   and set her shoe soles on the floor
and quite deliberately the lids which hide her eyes
draw back   I smile and wait   she mumbles and is still
eye talk creates alliance
yes   she wants to walk   I loose her bonds
remove the tray   invite again
she moves and stops   a fierceness in her eyes
(watch out   she hits)   her face invades my eyes
oh yes   as ill-used woman kisses me

SOCIAL WORKER JOURNEYS
INTO CHRISTMAS

❧

Cultured voice speaks rapidly
impulse on a wire from New York
well   I've been ill you see
my knee's replaced   I fell   remember?

in a pothole
and the city wouldn't pay a thing
oh dear it's hard and I can't see
and tell me   How is Pearl?

She's doing pretty well
and lady I can't save you
from the chaos in your mind or
hell outside your door

at least today
confusion's held at bay and
you are trusting me enough
to telephone

Pearl's in restraints again
and hollow eyed from Haldol
her staccato tearless sobbing
is occasional

Is this a family tradition
a path your New England ancestors trod
through the wilderness of time going
one by one around the glacial hills to madness?

She says   Oh I'm so glad   poor Pearl
It's Christmas and   oh dear
she must have something
toilet water   dusting powder   could you?

Of course, but can you tell me
who is helping you?
Do you have anyone at all?
(New York is not a place to go mad alone)

Oh yes   the priest is wonderful
I call him anytime and he helps me pay my bills
why yes   his number is
I have the clue I've sought for eighteen months

the primal thread's attached
to build a spiderweb
to catch and cradle
one more falling sparrow

oh God if that priest and I work
night and day from now to kingdom come
the web would never cradle her
at best we break her fall

so what will God's eye and a nickel buy?
and God you better watch her good because I'm not
one of your saints and I have four days off
for Christmas and the kids are coming home

COUPLE FOUND DEAD
STORED IN ATTIC
LINDEN, N.J. (AP) OCT. 31

&

I have suckled the wolf's lip of anger and I have used it for illumination,
laughter, protection, fire in places where there is no light, no food,
no sisters, no quarter.   - Audre Lorde

It's ha-ha-Halloween again
let's laugh and be scared
the paper says somebody's mom and pop
got petrified in a crawl space
laugh everybody

I don't want to laugh   I want to cry
petrifaction is not funny
I see folks turn to stone   a little bit
with every eyeblink   everyday
turn from person to tombstone
eventually the tombstone falls over but the funny part is
another body pops right up in its place and
with every blink that one becomes a bit closer to rock

And it's my job to fill the holes in the jack o'lantern's teeth
and keep the candle lit inside for warmth and cheer

never mind the wind's howling   that's only noise
the voices are quietened with pills for pain   for anxiety
          for rage much too large to be expressed

     So don't ask me to laugh at this newspaper clipping
               of old folks stored too long
          it isn't just Linden New Jersey   It's here
and everywhere there is age and pain   I don't care
          who means well and who means ill
          anyone old is at everyone's mercy   and
     there aren't nearly enough who are merciful
          put *THAT* in your Associated Press

HER PAIN

Circumstantiality to the trade
means irrelevant speech
but it's hardly irrelevant to Florence
who speaks thus:

Don't you know   yes   over there
he shouldn't have   last Tuesday
but we do   unless it's time for lunch
I'm glad   don't you?

The others turn away   or hurry past
leaving her mid sentence
slight shoulders down
eyes puzzled

HELLO HELEN

We will be   are   were
in an instant beauty becomes ugly

Somebody do something
give me a pill
call my son
no one will help me
oh God it hurts

We are all exposed
sometimes together
always alone
entering in motion
leaving in stillness
while a candle weeps

I visited sometimes
to hold your pain with you
it was very heavy
I meant to come back
but you didn't wait

And I am left wanting to be truer
more constant next time

FRANCES

❧

She is eighty-eight   blurred by stroke
a caricature of the roaring twenties redhead
who ate the big apple for breakfast
clear thinking risk-taker so savvy
she rose in publishing until
her decisions reached the White House

She says she is an immigrant
daughter of a Jewish junkman
quit school   bored   New York   two jobs
Columbia   success in several fields

She says she loved a brilliant man with two sur-names
who loved his work above her   so   she married
Charlie
and outshone him   he adored her
when he died   she never cried

Charlie never wanted anything but her
even the son she had at 35 because she didn't want to miss
motherhood

(only her son missed motherhood
but she didn't say that)   she said   of course
I had nannies   I never changed a diaper

She has come near the end to be with him
who doesn't quite have time for her

She says I don't belong in a place like this
it's absurd   what could I do here   nothing
I have no friends here   How can I live in a mill town?
no theater   no music   I'm not like these people

Her auburn bob is shaggy   long forgotten roots are white
her cheeks too red   her eyes deep set
are darkest tunnels to her mind
her mouth is wide   thin-lipped   her words
come out in bumpy rhythms   cooed low
like pigeons on a city street   sometimes
important ones vanish and she doesn't know
they never made it out at all

The world has tricked her   time has stolen
what she gathered by her wits
her fortune is in trust and she's on Medicaid
those to whom she cast her apple skins   are gone
or waiting now for her to go   and
with the wits she still has left   she knows
that he who laughs the last   laughs best

119

DECLARATION

What liberty is there in fear   in endless waiting
the inability to move?   would any adult American
or otherwise   surveyed in a supermarket sampling say
I've made my nursing home reservations
I can't wait to go?

The hell they would   with me
a million Patrick Henry's all declare
give me liberty or give me death

PREDAWN IN
THE NURSING HOME

She lies waiting for the night to be done
long after her private night
has opened again to consciousness
she is aware that   not yet but some time soon
total blackness will come
she sees shadows and the dull glow of a night light
shining through the siderails   and over there
someone   a stranger   still sleeps   still breathes
But she is alone   so single solitary   unattached
alone
where does she belong?   is everyone elsewhere but her?
she hangs   floats on this conscious brink of day
filled up with wanting   and forgetting   and
little clouds of remembered feelings   and vacant spaces
echoing and inviting
She is hungry for the day   for the faces
not the spaces
when will they come?   who came yesterday?
it's hard to remember

Today what faces will there be?   Which eyes
will pool themselves to hers?

121

        which hands will touch her?
soon?   which voice will call her thoughts to now
        from darkness into light?

No strangers please   no wounded angry ones   please
        no rough ones   distracted   in a hurry
    perhaps it will be someone young   with laughter
    rising up from her   like dawn   at least a smile
        to fill a bit of time   until the ticking stops

LEAF PILE

Autumn comes in silence
slowly
at the foot of trees
by night
The pre-dawn chill bleaches
random grasses
into glistening curves
silver sickles caught
in contemplation of
carving up the sun

Pods explode sparks
of living seeds
which travel epic journeys
with anonymous patience

Trees tense up
chilled to brittleness
sap thickens
oozes daily downward
clogs
leaves choke
ignite

There is so little beauty
in the dying of my people
in this lonely house of autumn

They who have been set apart
dry up
drop scarlet and golden dreams
reluctantly
ankle deep
at their own feet
to be carried away
and dumped into winter

A QUESTION OF PERSPECTIVE
1995

A hundred years from now
when some great progeny or other
discovers that I worked in nursing homes
I hope they gasp   the way I would today
to hear a relative of mine was in
the slave trade   or manned a German oven

PASTORAL VISIT

❧

The ancient child
delighted at my coming
stretches out her hand
grasping me
and holding

Her chin is bearded white
and curly   Hello
they cut my leg off   see
she bares the wizened stump and more
her one good eye drinks me in
the other milky blind looks over my shoulder at yesterday
or maybe tomorrow

I touch my chin
tweezed whiskers growing back
like fear

AT 36 — BILL

Wasn't ready   didn't wanna go
no how   no way
wanted to lay his wife wanted to go
fishin'   instead he drowned
in his own juices
later   the Baha'i ladies came
affirming God seven different ways
fifteen times apiece making waves
of sound to move him gently
from this life to the next
the one with the big teeth said
compare life to gestation -
in utero we are growing things
we can't use
why form lungs when you live in water?
why have eyes when you live in the dark?
nothing makes sense until
the bursting into light and air
nothing makes sense now except
affirming God   and trusting
the gentle lady with the big teeth

HOSPICE

Hospice is an idea
that death is natural not frightening or pitiable
and does not have to happen in a sterile and alien place

Hospice is a promise
twenty-four and seven
wherever you are you needn't be alone

Hospice is a hand to hold
a smile
a ragged breath made calm

a dance of leading and being led
always different   always the same
a choice for choice

Hospice teaches those who want to learn
how to live in the face of death
how to hang on   and when to let go

Hospice teaches how to look at past and future
how to be here in the moment
how to risk and be courageous

How to move ahead after failure
how to know success disguised as failure
and how to suspend judgment

Hospice is dealing
with shit and blood and tears
because of love

Hospice is finding that one shining needle
in a haystack of horrors
and being able to laugh

Hospice is life
rich abundant funny sad infuriating scary frustrating
wonderful
life at the end of life

A HEART WHICH DREAMS

CREED

I believe in water where I first began to grow
where now I am restored and come to play.
I believe in earth, the seed receiver,
waiting always ready to foster growth
who bears the journey of my feet
and bears the burden of my home;
It will receive my completed body

I believe in rocks which speak of time gone by
and of my true size in the scheme of things.
I believe in sunrise, sunset, tides and moon,
stars and seasons
whose regularity have taught me how to trust

I believe in God within every living thing —
that loving force
which programs life and sometimes leaves us free to choose.
I believe in my body which like the rocks bears witness
to time and events now unremembered.
I believe in emotion, child of the union of body and the
currents of the soul.

I believe in the gifts of the mind, but lightly, gingerly.
They tend to seduce.

I believe in the journey which my life is;
that it has meaning and purpose,
that I can make a difference while I'm here
to some around me
if I choose to love.

I believe I am here to learn to choose to love.
And I believe that suffering can blaze a trail to love
if properly received.
I believe that it is all right to die and that my body
will tell me the time... and after that...
it doesn't matter... what.
I believe what matters is now   and choosing love.

AN OLD ENGINE MISFIRES

Some of me was stolen in the night and I awoke afraid
at least I said something's wrong and as the day unwound
it rubbed my skin unmercifully
no   not my skin   my soul
was rather left impostured in my flesh
abrading me from inside out
I bore this all within awareness
moved as if I were myself
trusting that things change with time
trusting me trusting sleep trusting hidden dreams
and came the day a second time
and I was once more me

INSPIRATION

Picks it up the earth and gives it to me
It's he somewhere a walking...
-Mary Caroline Richards

After the sharing of hearts
beloved people move   leave   are called away
comes the letting go
comes the moving on before the stories done
I sometimes think this molecule of oxygen
I breathe may recently have come
from the lungs of a finch or fox
(do butterflies have lungs?)   a molecule
which I breathe out may find its way again
to someone I have loved
and they unknowing take me in again
Beware!   I will not let you go
I spin a spider's silk which binds
me to you and this   and this and you
so if antennae move
likely I'll receive the stirring
I do not forget we share this air
I answer with a bird song
or come as ruffled air against your cheek

BREATHING — A MEDITATION

Inhale
the mind of God

exhale
my busy mind

inhale
yes to the world as it is
expression of God in time

exhale
wants of mine that are not
meant to be just now

inhale
God's love bombarding me
with grace and opportunity

exhale
the good that I've received
back to the earth

inhale
the world into me

exhale
me into the world

inhale
God into me

exhale
me into God

AFTER DREAMING

With morning comes an absence
of wonders seen in microscopic purity
silken robes of glory held up   tried on
oh God   the colors

Mid-life a veil comes down on memory
the land of day has boundaries and customs
now to enter morning
my bags are searched for contraband visions

Only feelings are allowed through
the border guards are thorough
and I begin to understand why
old women sometimes choose to die

RADIATION THERAPY

Just after I learned to love myself
(which is another story)
I found a cancer in my breast
the one I cover to pledge allegiance
I am a medical social worker who used to
pledge allegiance to medical technology

I was   I think   pretty much a trooper
chatted with the surgeon at the biopsy
he's very sweet and has small children
his favorite surgery is bowels
they got it all at surgery he said
and all the nodes were clean

I know it's Russian roulette
else why the radiation therapy?
and all it takes is one breakaway cell
It's clear what must be borne

I think it was being positioned just so
and then abandoned   that raised up terror
the stunning aloneness   like death
all right!   sock it to me!   this can be borne

138

But don't ask me to suck up to that bitch of a nurse
or her tentative nervous smile   (the terror turns to rage
it's easier that way)   my venom could have killed her
I froze her out   flicked her off as if she were a leech
killed her many times inside my head   outside my head I
killed her with kindness   with fine thank you's and
please
excuse me's   she   the focus of my wrath

I wore the prim long-necked slightly smiling condescension
my mother taught as last ditch defense
kept to myself the memories of Hiroshima's children
for a full moon cycle and more

I remember making a mammary Christmas card
for the radiation techs   it wasn't their fault I was there
saw the doctor once   it was all math to him
when it was over he said to see him in six months time
said he wanted to know how I was doing   I did not
believe him
he wanted my money   fit consort for the bitch

I am usually nice   but always there was
a temper running through me
like molten lava a quarter mile down
couldn't ever let it out
life depended on going along

Years later I still ask myself
how dare they even think for an instant that

I would not *mind* having my body permanently tattooed
        just a little   for their convenience

    They used a magic marker instead   it sufficed
        in a way it didn't matter anymore
    terror   rage   these things tattoo the soul
I was only sunburned outside   inside I am scorched

THE FLY

🪰

The window of the present moment is raised
between panes a fly crawls
over   down   up   up to freedom
now able to fly off into the dim hallway
but seeing light   it will not settle
for anything less   it pushes on the glass
trying to break into the day

Past   present   future
I do not want ever
to go back into darkness
I am as hungry as the fly
for light   for future
for God

SMALL THINGS WRIT LARGE

I
The morning sun still hides
behind the newly naked wood
frost teeters on extinction's brink

squirrel sits   peeling   turning
lusting
for the peanut in his paws

I see his breath come out
a cloud of vapor like my own
but very small

and blessing his wee gluttony
I wonder
if I might befriend my own

II

A silhouetted crow on barren branch
turns wary head just so
and suddenly the eye becomes a brilliant star

Against that dark bird's cornea the sun's first rays
are angled to my retina   it's only
just geometry at work   but

It feels as holy as midsummer's dawn
seen through an ancient keyhole made of stone   and
as playful as God's eye caught winking just for me

TRANCE WORK

There is a passageway within
at will   I leave the day behind
slip easily down   around   through   rock
(made of who knows what — perhaps
remains of other lives)
I go deep   beyond sound to
utter safety where the mother is
Greek and beautiful
hair soft coiled above large eyes
I am only newly slim from babyhood
coltish joy-filled naked
capable of anything with her
We are deep within
the grotto curves above around
beneath us warm rock shelf
light dances on the walls above
beside us   the waters
of a luminous pool   core of divinity
Here at Sophia's spring I am being taught
I can ask my questions   be heard
be answered   be loved   BE
be enough   just as I am   be connected
to source   to wisdom   to tender caring

I see in these waters   in her eyes
the treasure that I am
We play at water's edge
I want to swim   she smiles and nods
I move as well as any seal and rolling
arc in curves of joy
burst forth and dive again laughing
into silence surrounded supported
go deep trailing bubbles
deeper   light grows dim   is gone
at bottom I explore a membrane with my fingertips
draw back   no fear   but knowing
this is not the time   the time
will come when I shall beat the membrane
like a drum with persistence
let me in   let me out
let me in   let me out

This then is death   saying no!
I cannot stand this separation from love any longer
and coming to the pool to her and slipping in
with joy at never leaving   ever
and breathing out and going down   straight down
swimming hard but smooth as satin
feeling every bit of it
down and dark and searching for the membrane
finally breaking it   breaking free
breaking water   borning into eternity
pulling bloody life behind me like an afterbirth
glad that it's not needed anymore

AFTER LIFE-THREATENING ILLNESS

If Jesus loves his suffering children
then what does it mean
not to suffer? not to be ill   undergoing therapies
losing hair   vomiting
the meaning seeps out of healthy bone
once treatment's done
and I am left confused   abandoned   disappointed
wanting so to be the acceptable sacrifice   to do life well
to do death well
do dying well   the primitive beliefs are hard
to purge   surprise!
One more time I must be taught the invalidity of sainthood
the subtle   hidden   powerful   sly   God
who always wants
more than I have to give   is once more unmasked
Trickster   Fraud   Liar   Thief
You steal me from myself
enslave me to hopelessness   I'll never be good enough
chain me to hope   maybe You'll love me anyway
get me begging to jump through fiery hoops
and hating myself

killing myself with the effort to please you
You God of my training
they say You created hell
but I'm the one who keeps on trying to jump in

THE SUNDERLAND SYCAMORE

This thing set random root and opened leaf
unnoticed in the virgin forest
grew patiently cell by cell
in almost silence

Grew roots out and down
enough to grip and hold the earth
fiercely
for eighty thousand days

And now this ancient being
each branch a full grown tree
dappled smooth reaches out
to catch the rising of another sun

Other trees are fully leafed
but here the sky melts down and air moves freely
through fat buds opening quite deliberately
the way an elder elephant might blink

This being inhales spring
and exhales autumn

pausing just to be
in the momentary winter

This one so long alive is holy
this sycamore   *sic amor* —
such is love
enduring

MEDITATION ON AN OLD CARROT

From the dark and cold
and out of plastic at last
a carrot kept too long
speaks to me
Root tufts
fine as facial hair
sprout everywhere
beauty is irrelevant
in the face of such intent
When I am very old   I hope
I still can send out
roots to nurture
dwarf pale and waxy
shoots that could go green with sun
And finally scraped and chopped
and in the boiling pot
let me nurture more
than I could ever dream

TELEPATHY WITH A MOLLUSK

Near Boston in October at a workshop
from a basket passed around
I chose a scallop shell
to take away

It says to me
the light is naked and dry
everything is lost without water

The clean perfection of precisioned lines
became anchorage
for barnacles   irregular   random flowerings
hung from cantilevered ribs

It says to me
I thirst for thick emerald light
shining through seaweed

Hard dry remnant kindles awe in me
in this dark and alien moment

I will just continue to be who I am
Even under the sea you mollusks know about moonlight
and moonlight proves the sun still shines

AFFIRMATIONS

I am of the earth   and the earth is good
I am of the sky   and sky is filled with light
I am of the ocean   deep powerful alive
I am a maple tree   well-rooted on a gentle hillside
with my arms thrown wide to life
I am a breeze   in love and touching
every single thing gently
I am rain falling   subject to wind   subject to gravity
letting go   falling free   life-giver
I am thunder   rolling sounds   proclaiming power
I am lightning   shining
on a golden journey at just the right speed

I sing out my name   The trees hearing it blossom
the words of another cannot speak my truth
I am a large-eyed child   utterly lovable   grown wise
I am the finger of God   light streams from me

MEMORY

I am a bag lady   forever
slipping down an alley to repack
weighing every single thing   often
is it really worth lugging this around?

I take nothing for granted
the dogma is gone   these days I seek
hypotheses   keep needing bigger ones
outgrow them like the shoes on old and spreading feet

Relentlessly my history slips away
a line of smallest bubbles rising
slow leak in me
who is submerged in life

He says   We've seen that film
or   You've been there
(sometimes I reach inside
to emptiness)

There is no going back to clarity
that exact awareness of my youth

I am only saved by habits
and small notes strategically placed

God will have to track my journey
from certitude to ignorance
from cotillions to the bliss of
watching bare trees move in winter

I cannot recall the source of yesterday's pain
or what wise insight came to me last week
my history is a shallow sea   and clarity
depends upon the wind

Yesterday's wisdom evaporates   who cares?
I am most surely marked by efforts of this life
in each moment   by intent and choice
I sculpt this fragment of eternity

ZIZEL BREAD*

❧

For Gus and Paul

It takes an hour down and back on a six lane road
and then a weave through suspect neighborhoods past
run down shops with forty percent off and all sales final
past decaying mansions to the city's other rim to find
the Jewish bakery and the Zizel bread

Two days a week they bake it   I see the satiny
textured things
large rounds upon the high shelf overlooking
the Boston cream pies   the finger cookies
dipped in chocolate
I buy three loaves and on the way home
the smell of it in the car
lets me wonder if perhaps I'd whore for it
You think like that driving through these streets

I am not a lady anymore   and this is not a bread
for tea sandwiches
this solid bread requires a sharp knife and muscle
it is a heavy crusted rye laced thick with caraway
each bite a small battle to rip the crust from itself

each rip a small victory over starvation's possibility
the chewing is work   releases explosions of flavor
of wholesome grains sun-warmed autumn days
picnics and laughter

In Eastern Europe the daughters of Abraham knew
surviving childbirth was the least of their problems
life was subject to random chaos   horses   swords
one mother   on a certain day
kneaded love and strength into a loaf
fired it   drew it out   tapped it   smelled it   cut it
and smiled

I get to take it home   It's quite unjust
It should be airlifted over these mean streets
and dropped by parachute everywhere   a lot of it
enough so all who struggle here
could feel the love and eat and then grow strong

*(pronounced "schissel")

THE CRONE DINES OUT
WAY OUT
❧

In my sixty-first year
for the very first time
I ate sweetbreads

Mother said
they're *organ* meats dear
you wouldn't like them

She never said which organ
and being me
I just assumed the worst

In my Montana days
Rocky Mountain oysters were everywhere
but in my mouth

You wouldn't like them dear
at last gave way
to me as part of sisterhood

These sweetbreads were fit for the gods
exquisite   why did it feel like a victory?
have I been at war?

Isn't there a rule somewhere   women who eat sweetbreads
shall be burned at the stake   a part of me believes
for such a trespass I should be beheaded

Sweetbreads with a glad and laughing sauce
they were tender as a maiden's longing for love
odd that the bull's fire streams from such a delicate source

The blood no longer runs between my legs
the living that was such an effort
has become a freedom   a fearlessness   a joy

She dines on sweetbreads who repudiates
control   domination   force   and rage
sweetbreads with a glad and laughing sauce

Methought to swallowed the origin of wars
the source of slobbering lust
I took them like communion

Not really   but in retrospect
it could have been a lovely ritual
thus shall ye know ye have become the crone   except

She who meant to dine on the fountain of creation
unknowing nibbled pancreas   and learned
what crones do best   is laugh

COMING OFF THE VENT

For Joyce

We scramble for technology when the body breaks down
surprised again that we are mortal fragile bleeding things
containers for a brain which rarely grapples with mortality
the brain so wants to run the show   you know

But even the brain has a master   psychologists have said
all cognitive functions are in service of affective interests
feelings move us   like the chain which grabs the roller
coaster car
hauls it up and up before the plummet into dying

It takes a wise one to know the spirit which generates the
feeling
that hidden connection to expression of divinity
Spirit knows the body is just a tool which serves awhile
and wears out exactly when the silent soul needs to fly

FIRST DAY OF AUTUMN

Trees grow upside-downward into sky
reflecting on the still bog water
and spawn themselves into reality
up where I am flying
on the bike path in the woods
so glad to be alive
in such clarity
and clean goodness
I want to turn me inside out
let every pocket in my soul
take the air
to better know
this brief and brilliant joy

ENIGMA

On the bike path through the woods
I watch for creatures while I fly
a bird   squirrel   snake
you never know what will appear

Up ahead six inches from the weeds a chipmunk waits
Hi guy I say approaching fast
still frozen   statued   he runs
exactly the wrong direction

A wheeled leviathan   a death machine   that's what I am
I feel that tiny bump with every nerve
I cannot bear to stop and look   pedal on
hard   cringing
hit and run   how could you not   even   stop?

Did the spinning of the silver wheels confuse him
the way a silver school of fish befuddles predators?
or was he ill   rabid   fevered?
what small dark place will not be warmed again?

And I who did not stop
to better know his loss
now contemplate a poem
as marker of his absence

HOUSE BLESSING 471 BAY ROAD

🌶

For Joan and Obediah

May this house be first and always
the home of spirit
a place where dreams may take on flesh

where comfort soothes
where beauty heals
and peace abides

May all who enter here
feel welcomed   safe enough
to set all artiface aside

Who live here   may they
grow and blossom
doing truth in love

ON HANG GLIDING

Feeling safe and not alone
I dare to contemplate
outrageous things
hang gliding off a mountainside

You hold the string
on this small kite you know
your quiet presence noticing
fills me with possibilities

This little boat would stay afloat
without you
ah
but having you as centerboard
I skim ahead
leaning into wind

RAINBOWS

GRATITUDE

I waken in the morning
ready curious open
life has been trustable

my eyes rejoice in weather
earth moods
to feed a hungry soul

my ears receive
the wind chime's song
or comments from a winged thing

my voice does not need to speak
the fingers write
the heart sings

JUST ANYONE

*

"In some of the fiction of South African writer, Bessie Head, the ambition of her characters is not to be extraordinary or considered extraordinary but to become 'just anyone'. which is perceived as the correct relationship to other people and the world. I feel this is also a correct alternative to despair, or, in some cases, suicide"   -Alice Walker

I am just anyone
no difference between me eating soup
and the next one my sister
my fingerprints lie all fingerprints
are washed away

all fingerprints pressing
on the glass leave trails of
oil for snails to track in curliques
ending dizzy or befuddled
falling off

my fingerprints are snails' trails
my smile the curve between the mountains
my breath whispers goodnight
in the seashell of my baby's ear and
the echo sets leaves shimmering

MY GOD

🥀

Make no assertion about God which you could not make
while standing over a pit of burning babies   - Elie Wiesel

There is no God
in the sky
waving our beseechments
left or right

No God
triumphal marching as to war
in the land of war most surely
God is not

There is no God
passing out tragedies
to soften us or toughen us
or break us

God is no
monster
no

Whom I call God
weeps tears of blood
beside the pit
of burning babies

LIEF

❦

Lief, Lef, a[O.E leof = D. lief = G. lieb = Goths liufs, dear;
the root of E. love] Archaic. Beloved or dear, glad or willing.
- *The New Grolier Webster International Dictionary of the English Language*

For a long time I thought it was about loving
just (at least) one other person really well
(because after all   any fool can love the whole world)

I wasn't wrong exactly   but it comes clear
the first allegiance is to be and say myself in truth
to hold my own spirit dear   beloved

Then comes the gladness and the willingness
to rise and greet the day
then comes the hope   to find and be with
those who know the truth
then comes the trust   not in rules or Jesus
but in me

I belong to this ecology of loving
I who was the missing puzzle piece
take my place at last in the family of things

BUBBLES

🐦

for Thessaly Rhiannon
my first grandchild

Once long ago
God said I want some people
and God made us   just like that   (more or less)

The way you say
I want to blow some bubbles
and you take soap and a big breath and there they are

Well   every single thing is bubbles
made from God's breath
shining   catching light   quite wonderful

with little bright windows
they mount the breeze   and fly
then pip   all gone   and what of that?

When you blow bubbles
and they burst
you smile and make another one

170

when God's bubbles burst my dear
all around us is
God's breath for cushioning

ADOPTION REVISITED

My daughter never caused me pain
I did not born her   we were introduced
how do you do my precious child   let me smell you
God yes!   I want you   yes I want to watch you grow

A generation later she bears fruit this gentle woman
waits a little nervously for pain I never felt
she's filled to bursting with another life
she ripens like a melon in a sunsplashed field

Mrs. Morgan requests the privilege of being present
at her grandchild's birth   it would end imagining
it would be she adopting me you see
finally I could know a birth through brailling hers

I want to say hello   give promise
of forever love to a new
still slippery splendor

LETTER TO MADISON ROSE

I did see her birth

A year ago you were about to *be*
I saw your slippery splendor born
and then the earth spun on   spins still
astonishing me   after all these autumns
and all these surprises

Yesterday early the sky was domed in rolling pewter clouds
I was in a giant lidded bowl not yet sealed
and only at the rim of the world was clarity
and as I drove to work a giant sunrise klieg light
from behind
proclaimed show time

Ahead   a pale and brittle cornfield and beyond
the hillside just beginning to undress for winter
the wardrobe crimson saffron cinnamon was flagrant
against a slender slice of clear sky
awestruck I stopped my car

Child   what I want to tell you is
something you know now   but the world

will try to seduce you into forgetting as you grow
you must live in the world
but never forget the earth

After many years of truths learned
and unlearned it is the earth I trust
that speck among the stars flung
like a handful of sugar across
a black and shining floor

That one speck a jewel
have you seen the picture   earthrise
taken from the moon?   the seas   the swirling clouds
I try to gauge my problems in the light of it
we each of us is very very small
and splendid beyond telling   worthy of birth
made to see and recognize spirit
on a hillside afire on a Tuesday morning
made to dream and hope
and best of all to love

Take time my daughter's daughter
just to be   to feel your spirit in your skin
and when you need replenishing look to mountains
craggy places   streams trickling   oceans exercising
find a microscope and really see the moss
don't miss a rose petal magnified
let the rain fall on you   make beauty in a garden

find where the squirrel lives and feed him
respect other lives
no matter the size   remember   earthrise from the moon
remember *all* spirits are at once great and small

I SAY

Hooray for mystic rebellious fools who say
God speaks from your heart   to your heart
be still   listen   learn   trust yourself
recognize
that to be human is beautiful   it is to be a flame
we each are God's energy burning
there is nothing apart from androgynous divinity

an atom in a speck of wood is mostly empty
vast space
a few electrons fly around a nucleus
I am only space energized to life
the wedding of divinity to clay

MAKING WORLD

Suppose
that it is we who generate
grace for each other

If I could really love
who knows where in the world
a blessing might be felt

I think it matters here
and somewhere there (for balance)
exactly what I do

An act done well might raise up grace
to be a bandage
for a wounded world

Maybe God is just the knitter
knitting patches for our world
with wool that we provide

Or maybe God is like a railroad switchman
just trying to keep the train going
where it is needed for a healing

When I am callous thoughtless maker of a wound
perhaps the world entire groans
for good or ill it seems no one of us lives alone

RUMINATIONS

I wonder
do they wait in winding lines to come in
those souls before they get to earth
is it like going to the theater?

Do they have a choice ?
which show to see
(we surely do get lost in)
farce or stress-filled dramas

Did I choose   America   1935?
like buying a first class ticket
on a queen
(Elizabeth or Mary)

What paid the price?
the suffering of another life
mine   or someone elses or
did I win a lottery to be lucky me?

Have I ever   been free?
I used to think so
but it feels true   that bit I read

about our thinking we are free

When all we really do is
rearrange the grass and straw
within our little box
and call that choice

Or possibly
I really am   free
held down in place by my imaginings
of walls

I love the play   have come to love the earth
so much the final curtain seems a tragedy
unless I see with cosmic eyes
the goings on in this small corner of the world

I will applaud   and call bravo
for the beauty in this little tale
no matter what comes
after this theater

A limousine ride or too long a walk
down cold and empty streets
until I am run over or mugged or
otherwise finished once and for all

Or will I then awake
and clap again and cheer
for the reality
of the play outside the play?

AFTER HARA BREATH WORK*

It isn't all sweetness and light you know
I am strong enough to break your bones
so don't cross me Buster

You stand for all those breath sucking fellas
who danced me to exhaustion
round and round and spat me out as not enough

Well I'm enough now by Christ
and if you don't believe me just
set your foot over the line

Stay on your own side and I will smile
or sing or cook for you or even love you
but tread on me and you're history

Because my grandma was a sumo wrestler
and my mother was a linebacker
and I bet your daddy wore a tutu

---

* Going from side to side, lunging in and out of the squat position with elbows bent
and hands up while bringing forth the sound *Huh* from deep in the belly

RETIREMENT

I was taught to be   carefully trained to be   unworthy
was schooled in striving   setting limits   living up to shoulds
for a lifetime I   did the right thing

Like the little piggies   I went to market   stayed home
ate roast beef   had none   as earnestly as I could
spent a lifetime earning my way until

the voice of love whispered   why not?
let go   free fall   liberate yourself
flirt with decadence   take the last piece   savor the moment

Swept along by waves of applause
I have fallen down a rabbit hole at the other end of life
it's a queer place this Wannaland

There are no rules except the ones I make
Sunday might be Tuesday   or Monday
could be Saturday night

There is no need to get to bed   I can sleep in
or rise at four and nap at two
there are delicious options for the mind and for the heart
Rain thumples down the drain pipe at the corner of the house

I know how a raindrop feels   and like the last little piggy
the task now seems to be   to cry whee whee whee whee
all the way home

HEART TO HEART

You have come so far little one   but you are not yet home
now is the time for different softer learning
how to be

How to let a day slide away   so you are surprised
when it is gone
surprised but not caught short
to know that what you did was enough because
there was no resentment in your heart
just taking in a yes to this and this and this   which is
not needing other to be anything more than it is
not needing change   just saying ahh
this is this   and that is that
and no one is keeping score

You are a jewel   a joy   perfect
sitting in the middle of your imperfection
and loving the spot   knowing perfection is a mirage
a lie
knowing that it is about being   and letting be
about blowing a kiss when you can and keeping
a prayerful heart
even when you don't know God's name

There are some things yet to come   but you will
                    weather them
         with a softness you are learning now

              Take a lesson from the listening trees
                    stretch   but gently
         you can be a long silver ribbon   like a river
you are here now   and you are on your way to the sea
                    it is all one

DECEMBER THOUGHTS

Most of the time we think there's nothing out there
just sky   (which is miracle enough)
very long ago the news was so good
angels excited themselves to visibility and song

There've been no reports of angels lately
although there was a trend   made millions
lately the sky is cold and dark
and current news is nothing angels celebrate

One theory says all creation is moving slowly upward
rock to plant to animal to human to angel
what if angels are humanity's graduates
everywhere around us in the air like plankton in the sea

Encouraging   praying   weeping
listening   protecting
teaching   hovering like a birthing coach
trying to help us breathe through trials
speaking calmly the way to journey home

HAPPINESS

Why do I want to apologize
to the world
because life is so sweet?

I tell myself
it is no crime
to be happy

Many   many
deserve but do not
have what I have

Old woman hopes
happiness is like salt in the stew
intensifying the flavor of life for everyone

CHRISTMAS EVE

I have arranged the treasures of the years
the Santa in his velvet coat   the crayoned angel primitive
and candles enough to set the world ablaze

But Santa will not come tonight   there are no children here
their lives are elsewhere   they have Christmas trees of their own
to decorate   and babies to dazzle

This night of wonder is about absence
of those trusting small faces   of surprise and hubbub
it is the absence of giving which is hard

But there comes a time to let it go
and the gift of giving is theirs now
it will make them strong

They will visit late in the week   come over winter roads
in hours-long trips   with cars packed full
when stress lets go its strangle hold

And I will lay open my heart   my tiny home
will bulge with babies and disorder   I will feed
them with roast beef and German chocolate cake

They will sleep in   laugh and play   show off their progeny
    and down inside wonder if they are good enough
        they are   their imperfections are exactly right

    This holy eve   he and I will spend a quiet night
        doing the usual things   and thinking about
            what it all means   this love

We have so much   have lived so much   we need no gifts tonight
        the gift is   that there are two of us
            and we are at peace

PUZZLES

*

What kind of a God creates a world
of infinite possibility and then allows
spokesmen to say
God lives down a one way street?

What kind of a God creates a world
where big things eat little things
so that smaller things must live in wariness
which sometimes and finally blossoms into terror?

I am made of minerals plants
and other sentient beings
the clucking hen the silver fish
and creatures herded to my need

Barbarous   yes
unless we all belong to each other
help each other up the ladder of being
meet at the top as equals some day

The poet Rumi says we lived and died
as minerals and plants and animals
thousands of years for each
before we ever learned to read

Sufi mystic wondered what we ever lost by dying
it will be at least a thousand years
till I become an angel   I see too much   am ill at ease
perhaps too newly shorn of fur and feathers

All men are not created equal   too many
never have a chance   ignorant babies
having ignorant babies   one more dream
terminally tattered on a pile of trash

The eye in search of food
has little patience with art
I am a lucky one   I live with beauty
feed the squirrel   have time to wonder   and write

It is important to live well
How?   send out love
ease pain   savor beauty
ah   but in what proportions?

This life is not a contest
or a race to the top of the ladder first
I hold hands with rocks and dirt
and everything between them and me

A Prayer: may salt become a lettuce leaf
the beet a baby lamb
carrot turns to running mare
wise one into seraphim

I don't want to go to God alone
I think I'd like to fly without a body
whisper a while in an open ear
channel to a listener someday

I hold this planet with one hand
it rests between my shoulder blades
in the curve of my neck   I want to climb to God
with everything or nothing at all

WE THE DREAMERS

❧

Who would know to look at Homo Sapiens
that we are made to search the night sky
for light   for angels   for UFOs
that we are made to dream

But we are not the only ones
who wait with feathers on to dance in praise of light
all living hearts yearn for the ineffable
only hubris says that we alone dream worthy dreams

The cricket dreams of springing to a land safe enough to flaunt his song
appetitive mouse dreams tiny bits of flavored things
here and there   just for the taking
owls see surprising visions unknown to hairy things

Wolves' and coyotes' dreams make undulating song
in witness of the night and brotherhood
the silent deer reads poetry in the shimmer of a leaf
a snake dreams one unending curve containing everything

Every living thing dreams mightily
its particular image of more
it is the assemblage of our dreamings
which pushes clocks to tick

THE BODY CAST

I see on the wall in her home a plaster belly
and sagging breasts
mounted on cloth with dried flowers
her belly then was filled with child

My breath goes deep   is like the sea   whispering
between my ears as it slips down the lining of my throat
through the clever cautious opening to the vital place
wherein all of me rests in the chalice of my pelvis

Breath stirs all that is contained within like a rich soup
and like the sea I lap against the boundaries of skin
back and forth slowly gently as my limbs are nourished
spine rises tall   carries vision and sound back
to the soft stew of dreams   regrets   hopes
and knowings

I want to make a body cast of plaster   my belly
never swelled like that   ripe as a plum fit to burst
that golden plum was never mine who yearned
so totally for it
but over the years I think I grew large enough
to forgive that old absence

194

I cannot imagine who could tolerate my body the way
I have come to
it is my faithful servant   not pretty   but used
to my ways
and willing to do my bidding
I wish to rejoice in it   enough to make a plaster cast
Would I dare to ask my friends to come
and fit the warm and slippery wet over my nakedness
body hair and purple spider veins and cellulite
so my tired friendly sagging rumpsprung self
could know itself appreciated?

I will to put my love on every bruised and broken place
I will raise it up on good black velvet
with poppies blood red   and cornflowers
cobalt blue bending down in homage on the wall because
I will miss it when I leave   I know I will
how can I know myself without it?

I think who I will always be is
the big-eyed kid at the bake shop window
the kid gurgling laughter as the roller coaster roars down
the kid squatting over a puddle gently moving the stick
to see what water does   the kid barely touching moss
so filled with earth love I may never be able to go home

But I will go home finally because home   wherever that is
is where the hugs are always waiting and are so large
and good

that all my boundaries melt away
the river of soup which I have been   will pour
with no reticence at all   into the sea of what is

ON HOLOGRAMS AND HEALINGS

A hologram is a three D picture
made of something real
It's not just smoke and mirrors

The tiniest fragment of a hologram
when put to lazer light
produces the complete hologram again

Each of us is a fragment of God
sometimes we can make God real
for others

Suppose there is no God   *out there*
suppose the godding happens here
in us   between us

(Everyone *says*
God is love
don't they?)

I stopped believing long ago
in a Nielsen rating God who looks down to see
how many are praying for rain

I prayed to be aligned with God's will
I prayed in gratitude
that's all

But now the *Utne Reader* says in double blind studies
on heart attack patients   more people died
in the control group without prayer
and they define prayer as   love sent out

I want to be
the tiniest fleck of the hologram
true part of true whole

I set out
with glad heart
to make love

A SPLENDOR OF THIS LITTLE LIFE

Are you all right? he says   tapping on my door
  four-thirty in the morning   my light is on
              the moon wake you?
  m-m-m-m I say   a poem   come listen
      Old man turns sleepily   goes off
  comes back with pillows   snaps the blanket on
            climbs in to listen

        It is the elegy for my little brother
            it makes me cry again
              m-m-m-m he says

        Then we draw close together
          his hand holds my breast
          my fingers rest in his hair

GOD SEED

....There is a tidal pull toward potentiality, wholeness,
the intent of the seed - as a hazelnut becomes a hazel tree
so a God seed becomes God   - Anna Richardson

It rings of truth that we are God seed
random scattered on the earth
blown by who knows what
over rock and desert

We drown
or land in fertile field
only come to guess what we are meant to be
with nurturing

We are called forth out of ourselves
to stand soul naked in moonlight
with this potential to become
which was programmed somewhere out beyond the stars

THE REACHING

Sometimes when I sit silent listening
for God
my breath takes on the rhythm of the sea

The rising of my chest becomes the wave
forming from the vastness of the sea
that powerful and rounding curve
which hungers for the beach
rears up until my lungs are gorged on air
and still   and still
my breath must choose to throw itself from off the cliff
of will

The exhale is chaotic bliss   a letting go
an effervescent sand-filled sea which roils itself uphill
at last to beach
until momentum dies
and it must sink again between the grains of sand
to hide
so very wanting not to go
must come to stillness must accept
retreat
to join the once more gathering of wave

THE LAST BEST HOLY CARD

❧

I've given up searching for God   out there
transcendence leaves me feeling somehow diminished
focuses me on what I am not
ignores divine spark   the energy
which fuels me into loving

I have become my own holy card
I look to my own sacred heart
open up the small twin doors to the furnace
in my chest and see divinity ablaze
and cupping near my hands I am warmed

WHAT HE WANTED

*

"We all need some touchstone, some simple act that helps center
us into a remembrance of what is whole and beautiful." - Wayne Muller

He was not afraid of solitude   was gifted   famous
and he loved these friends
who shared the holiday   the food

He knew he was probably leaving
knew this meal might never be repeated
no more laughter   no more waking them to themselves

He who was fully awake and loving them
did he think they might not understand   might forget
might go back to being small selves after all

He thought   eat bread   drink wine
everyone does that   all he said was
when you do this remember me

He meant remember me with these
the way the sunrise
reminds the birds to sing

He meant it is happening so fast
I am afraid I will die
hold on to me   don't forget me

He needed their little act to be a touchstone
he wanted to keep them all connected
in the remembering of what was beautiful

A holiday
a life among friends
who love each other

THE WISH

*

God
has never spoken to me
directly

Most of what has come to me
of the holy
has come through other people

So loving God
I want to live
that it could be said

She is
so
God must be

ABOUT THE AUTHOR
✍

Rosemary Ix Morgan wrote her first poem when she was nine and has been writing ever since. The poems in this book were written from the late '60s through 1997. They start in New Jersey during a difficult time, continue through a move to Montana in 1971, where the proverbial fresh start did not pan out and where her 17 year marriage ended. In 1975 Rosemary and her three children moved to Amherst, MA where she earned an M.Ed in counseling and became a licensed social worker, progressing from working in a nursing home to hospital oncology and ending with seven years as a hospice social worker before retiring at the end of 1996. Rosemary remarried in 1979 and currently has three grown children and two granddaughters. She continues to live in Amherst with her husband, Earl.